If you leave me tonight I . . . I . . . I . . .
I'm not going to be your friend!"

What Kind of Baby-sitter Is This?

written and illustrated by **Dolores Johnson**

SCHOLASTIC INC.
New York Toronto London Auckland Sydney

Copyright © 1991 by Dolores Johnson.
All rights reserved. Published by Scholastic Inc.,
730 Broadway, New York, NY 10003, by arrangement
with Macmillan Publishing Company.
Printed in the U.S.A.
The text of this book is set in 15 point ITC Zapf
International Light. The illustrations are rendered in
watercolor and colored pencil on paper.

ISBN 0-590-47092-2

1 2 3 4 5 6 7 8 9 10   08   99 98 97 96 95 94 93 92

To those who have helped me:

Nina Kidd
Deborah N. Lattimore
Kendra Marcus
Cecilia Yung

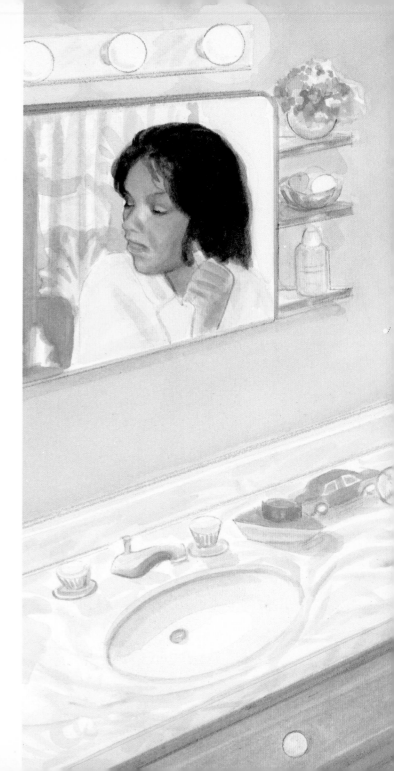

Kevin's mother was getting all dressed up to go out. And then the doorbell rang.

"Not another baby-sitter!" cried Kevin. "You said you'd take me with you next time!

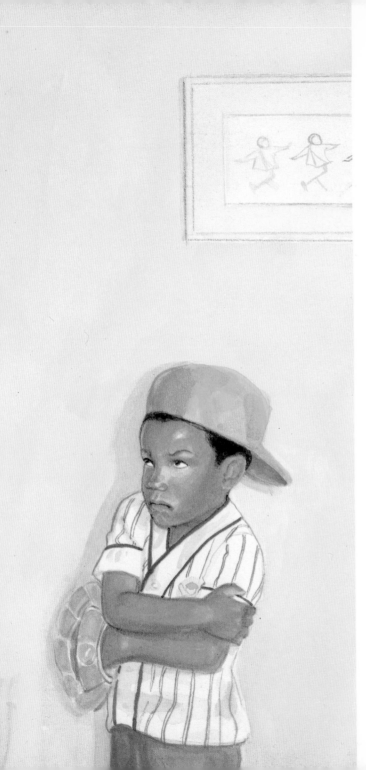

"Kevin," said his mother. "This is
Mrs. Lovey Pritchard. She'll take care
of you while I'm away at school."

"Take a look at that face, that sweet little face," said the baby-sitter. "You can call me Aunt Lovey, sugar dumpling."

"Mom, take me with you!" yelled Kevin.

"So you're the little boy who doesn't like baby-sitters," said Aunt Lovey. "Well, we're going to have such fun together."

"Mom, don't leave me with her, puullleeease!" yelled Kevin.

"Don't you worry about us, little mother," said the baby-sitter. "Kevin and I will be just fine."

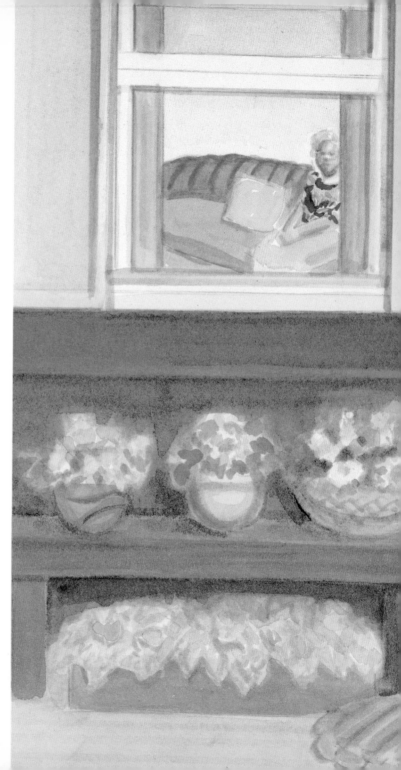

"Well, I'm leaving, too!" said Kevin as he stormed through the kitchen out to the back porch. "That old lady will never miss me. She'll be busy doing what baby-sitters do—painting her toenails, talking on the telephone, and eating the good stuff in the refrigerator. Hey, she'd better not eat that last piece of cake!"

Kevin sneaked back into the kitchen. "Isn't she even gonna come after me? Is that lady so dumb she doesn't even know I'm gone?"

From his hiding place, Kevin heard the click of a switch and then the roar of the television. "So that's what she's doing. She's watching soap operas. And my mom is paying her a zillion dollars to watch *me*."

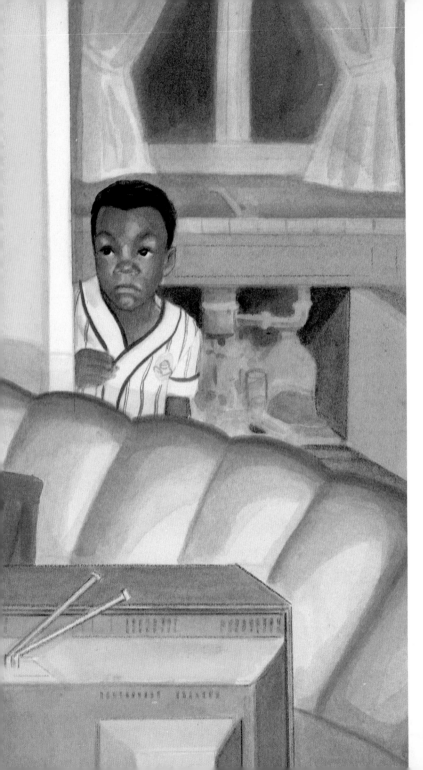

Aunt Lovey started yelling, jumping up and down, and clapping. "She's watching my baseball game! My *mom* wouldn't even watch it. What kind of baby-sitter is this? She's supposed to be yelling at *me*."

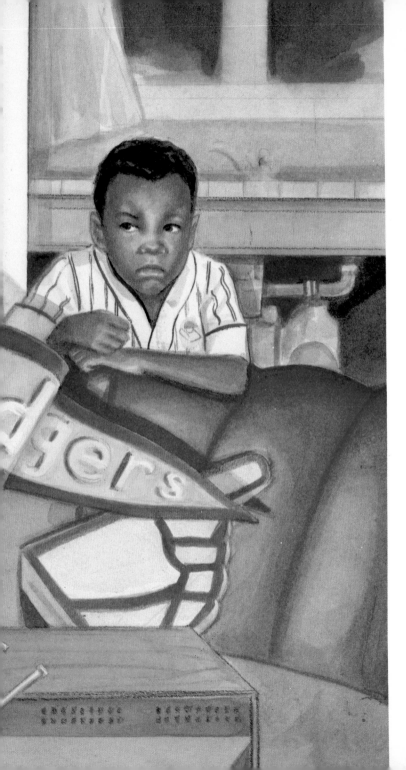

The baby-sitter started pulling
things from her handbag. She put a
baseball cap on her head. She laid
some baseball cards on the couch,
and she waved a pennant in the air.

"I wish she would put that pennant
down," said Kevin. "I can hardly see."

"And it's a Badger pennant," con-
tinued Kevin. "That proves it. She
doesn't know anything about baseball.
Everybody knows that the Badgers
can't win."

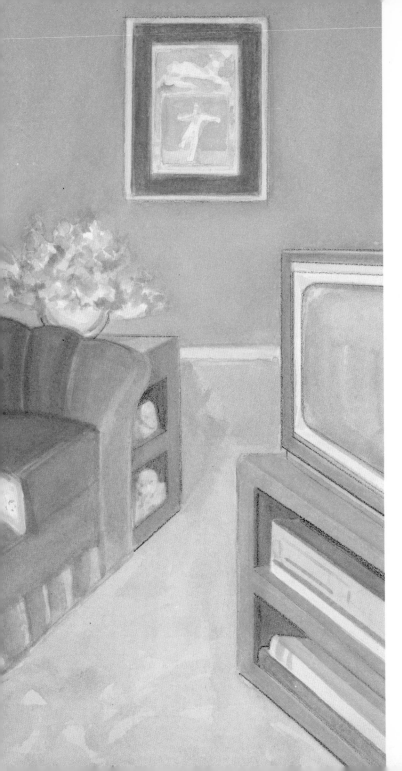

When the ball game ended, and the Badgers had won, Aunt Lovey turned off the television set. She was so busy pulling things out of her purse, it seems she never even noticed Kevin.

"Oh, no," said Kevin. "Here it comes now . . . her telephone numbers . . . her nail polish . . . those kissy-kissy books that baby-sitters read."

But Aunt Lovey pulled out a book about baseball, opened it, and began to read softly.

"I wish she would speak up," said Kevin. "I can hardly hear."

So Kevin crawled closer and Aunt Lovey read louder, and they read, and played games, and told jokes, and laughed so much that they didn't even notice when Kevin's mother came home.

"Are you still angry with me, sweetheart?" Kevin's mother asked when she came in. "I really hated to leave you. But, of course, there'll be other times when I'll have to go out."

"Well, that's all right, Mom, 'cause I've got a great idea," said Kevin. "Can Aunt Lovey move in with us? We can make her a bed on the couch, or she can share your bedroom with you. This can be her home, too."

"But, Kevin," said his mother, "Aunt Lovey has her own home. Baby-sitters don't stay over."

"Mom, you don't understand. Aunt Lovey's no baby-sitter— she's my friend!"